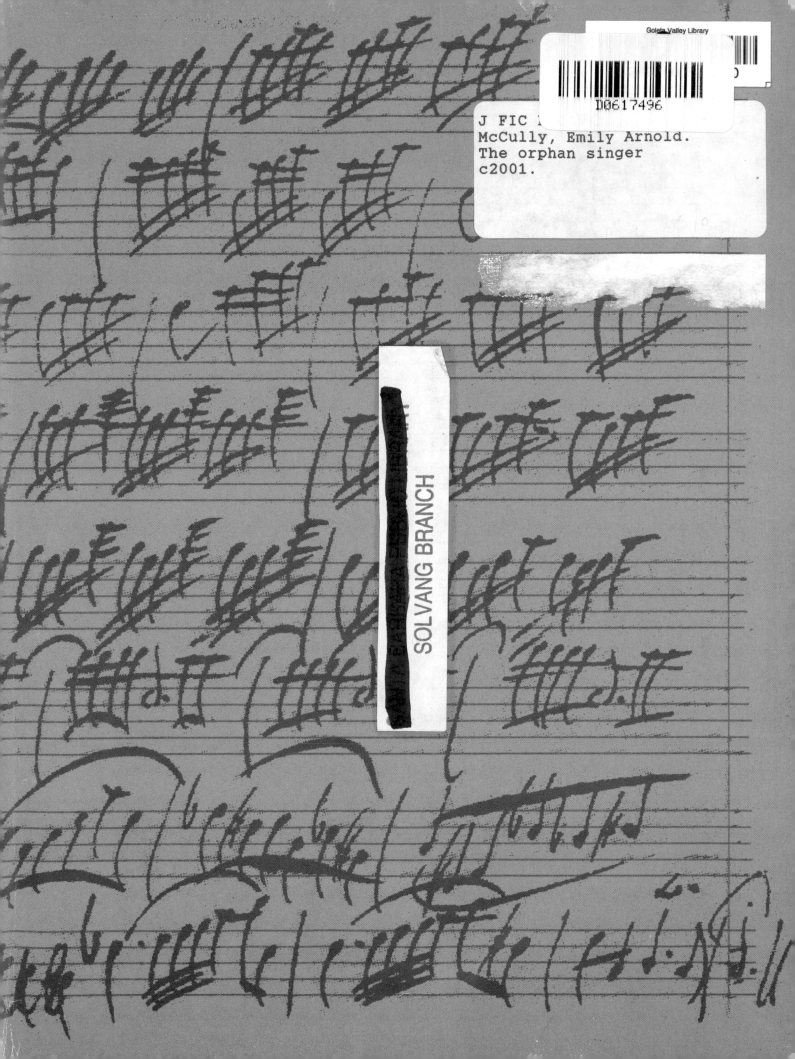

The Orphan Singer

WRITTEN AND ILLUSTRATED BY

Emily Arnold McCully

Thanks to Micky White for literally unlocking the Pieta
and sharing her discoveries about the figlie del coro.

OSPEDALO (oh-spay-DAH-lo): originally a word that meant a hostel for pilgrims, later an orphanage.
CAMPO (CAHM-po): public square

LIBRARY OF CONGRESS CATALOGING-IN-PUBLICATION DATA

McCully, Emily Arnold

The orphan singer / by Emily Arnold McCully.   p. cm.

Summary: Determined that their daughter realize her musical destiny, her poor but
devoted parents send her away as a baby to the Venetian 'ospedale,' knowing she will
be raised as an orphan and will never again be allowed to return home.

ISBN 0-439-19274-9

[1. Singing--Fiction. 2. Venice (Italy)--Fiction. 3. Italy--Fiction.] I. Title.

PZ7.M13913 Or 2001   [Fic]--dc21   00-063557

10 9 8 7 6 5 4 3 2 1   01 02 03 04 05

First edition, November 2001

Printed in Mexico 49

The artwork was done in watercolor and tempera.

The text was set in 15-point Hoefler Requiem.

Book Design by David Saylor

Arthur A. Levine Books

AN IMPRINT OF SCHOLASTIC PRESS

Like all Venetians, the Dolcis were musical. They had barely enough to eat but they sang from morning to night.

Little Antonio's sweet, clear voice could bring tears to the eyes of a passing grandee.

"If only we had money to send him to choir school or to a maestro for lessons," Papa Dolci would say.

"It's useless to think of what might have been . . ." his wife lamented.

Still, the Dolcis were reminded every day that Antonio would always be a basket maker.

When Nina was born, Antonio sang to her—and one day she sang back, giggling and burbling and cooing in harmony!

Antonio was ecstatic. "She is musical, like me!" But his parents were glum.

"How can we keep another child from its rightful destiny?" Papa Dolci asked. "A voice needs to be trained. It must be heard in the world. We will hardly be able to feed the child."

"Papa," said his wife, "what about the *ospedalo*? . . ."

In the *ospedalo*, foundling girls received the best musical training in Europe. But the school accepted only orphaned babies. Later, the talented ones were picked for the choral school.

"We would have to part from her forever!" cried Mama Dolci.

"But you're right. Where else can a girl get an education? How else can she be a musician?" said Papa.

"May we visit Nina there?" Antonio asked, through his tears.

"Once she has been trained," his parents promised.

So, with aching hearts, they left Nina in the infant drawer at the *ospedalo*.

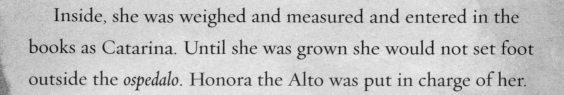

Inside, she was weighed and measured and entered in the books as Catarina. Until she was grown she would not set foot outside the *ospedalo*. Honora the Alto was put in charge of her.

This proved to be a demanding job. Catarina could disappear down some corridor in an instant. Sometimes she heard a boy's sweet voice singing a familiar song and she scrambled to the window to listen.

The Dolcis devoured any scrap of news about their Nina. From outside the *ospedalo* they heard the bells that rang to mark the day and they imagined her at school lessons, in the lecture on good behavior, during music lessons, doing her chores, eating meals, and sleeping.

When a new little girl was chosen for the choral school, word traveled fast and the Dolcis knew it was their Nina.

The older girls set out to train and stretch Catarina's angelic voice. She learned the scales and harmonies quickly. In no time she could sing impossible high notes and endless arpeggios.

She was still too young to take part in the famous concerts. But she could sit in the room where the girls received their admirers. The Dolcis were always there, straining to pretend they were strangers. One day, Antonio couldn't help himself and he started to sing Nina's song.

"It's you!" Catarina cried happily. "You sing to me from the canal!"

"You are our favorite of all the girls," Mama Dolci told her.

"Will you visit me again?" Catarina asked.

"We will always be here," Papa Dolci promised.

Catarina's teachers were astonished by her singing. But one of them, Apollonia the Soprano, was extremely strict.

When Catarina imitated a monkey playing the kettle drum, Apollonia was furious. "Catarina, you will never be asked to sing for the Maestro if you cannot be good!" she cried.

Still, Catarina whispered to Bettina during the lecture on good behavior and was made to eat bread and water for a day. When Catarina braided Maddalena's hair to her chair during prayers, Apollonia ordered her to wear the common girls' uniform for a week.

The Dolcis were alarmed by all this, but what could they do? "Try to be good, dear," Mama Dolci said gently. She was terribly worried that Nina might never be asked to join the chorus.

The Maestro had just finished a composition to be performed for visiting royalty. It was filled with impossible high notes and endless arpeggios.

"Send me the best new girls," he said. Apollonia had to send Catarina. She brought tears to the Maestro's eyes when she sang.

"I want her for the concert next week!" he said. "Hasn't she got a proper uniform?"

"But Catarina is not good," said Apollonia. "Goodness is a requirement of the board of governors!"

"She sings like an angel!" declared the Maestro.

The Dolcis had no money for tickets, so they joined the music lovers clustered outside under a window. Antonio was certain he heard Nina's pure soprano.

Afterward the Dolcis hurried to the reception.

"You will be a great diva," Antonio said. "It is assured."

"See how alike they all look," Maddalena remarked.

"It must be because they come so often," said Bettina.

Now that she was preparing for a concert every week, Catarina
tried hard to stay out of trouble. But she was so nervous sometimes
she just had to make faces at Paola!

"Shall you stay in your room during the concert?" Apollonia asked.

"But I am good!" Catarina blurted.

"Impudent!" cried Apollonia. "Any more mischief and you will pay!"

Catarina poured her high spirits into the performances. Soon the Dolcis were sharing their darling with other music lovers eager to meet her.

This was exciting for Catarina, but the only people she always counted on seeing were the Dolcis. She wasn't sure why. . . . The man and his wife and their son meant more to her than anyone.

Then one evening they didn't appear. Catarina listened impatiently to the chatter of people she didn't care about. Where were the Dolcis? She felt sadly abandoned.

Then Papa Dolci hurried in. "My child," he said.

"Where are Mama Dolci and Antonio?" Catarina asked.

Weeping, he told her that Antonio was very sick and sent Catarina his last good-bye.

She dragged herself to bed, but couldn't sleep. Antonio might die! No one was allowed to leave the *ospedalo*. But what did her music matter if Antonio were not there to hear it? If only she could sing to him now, wouldn't he hear her love and get well?

The corridors and the stairs of the *ospedalo* were empty. The door was locked tight.

But the porter had fallen asleep, and Catarina lifted a key from her lap.

At the *campo* she found a dozing gondolier and asked him to take her to the address the Dolcis had mentioned.

There was only the silvery sound of the dipping oar as they glided along.

It was strange to be out in the world for the first time. But Catarina paid little attention to that. She concentrated all her thoughts on Antonio. Make him well!

"Nina!" Papa Dolci cried when he saw her. Catarina didn't stop to correct him.

"Where is Antonio?" she cried.

Following him she thought, *How strange, I feel as if I have been here before.*

Antonio was so pale and weak. But when he saw her, his eyes brightened. Catarina started to sing his song. It was as if an angel had come to comfort them.

"I missed the concert," Antonio whispered.

"You must get well and hear the next," Catarina said. "I love you all so much."

She would be expelled from the chorus now. But how could she not have come? Antonio was like a brother, the Dolcis like parents.

The gondola delivered her to the *ospedalo* at dawn. Would angry Apollonia be there to meet her?

But the door was opened by Honora!

"Child! Where have you been?"

Catarina blurted her story. "I know I must leave the chorus," she said.

Honora looked into her eyes. "The governors require the girls to be good. You have shown that you are both good and brave," she said. "Go and do your chores. I will send word as soon as Antonio improves."

In a few days, Antonio had recovered and Catarina sang for the Maestro with a full heart.

She became a favorite girl of the chorus. Even gondoliers and street peddlers knew her name. But fame didn't go to her head. Catarina taught the younger girls with Honora's kindness.

When she was eighteen, the impresario at the opera invited her to perform. This led to a triumphal tour of the other great opera houses of Europe.

She was able to provide for the Dolcis. She even took them to the countryside every summer for their health. The Dolcis' dreams for her were now real.

And their daughter had long since guessed the truth.

Author's Note

IN THE EARLY EIGHTEENTH CENTURY, when this story takes place, the state of Venice supported four welfare institutions for orphaned and abandoned girls, each with a superb music conservatory. Strict obedience to rules of living was enforced by the governing board of each *ospedalo*. The institutions operated autonomously, earning income from concerts and sales of scores, as well as from silk laundering operations, lace-making, and other enterprises. They had existed for hundreds of years, one accepting homeless children, another the sick, and at the Pieta, only foundlings. The infants were introduced there, sometimes with a note, through a revolving door set into the wall called a *scarfetta*.

Girls in the Pieta were selected for the chorus and orchestra schools at as early as three years of age. They wore red uniforms, enjoyed special privileges, such as extra firewood and lamp oil, and trained rigorously for the famous concerts. These concerts were attended by the music-loving citizens of Venice and were must-see destinations for tourists when the city was the pleasure capital of Europe.

The older girls taught the younger ones, the pyramid capped by a hired maestro. Vivaldi was Maestro for many years at the Pieta, composing for girls whose individual talents he knew and could challenge to ever greater heights. Many girls sang and were *virtuosi* on more than one instrument. The music was performed from balconies in the chapel, the girls hidden by iron grills for the sake of decorum.

Everyone in Venice knew the girls by their first names and compared their merits along the canals and in the *campos*. The girls were encouraged to remain in the *ospedali* for life, but some left when they were grown up for careers in opera, and some married. Refuting the idea that women are not naturally gifted composers, the *ospedali* produced many: ten in the *New Grove Dictionary* alone.

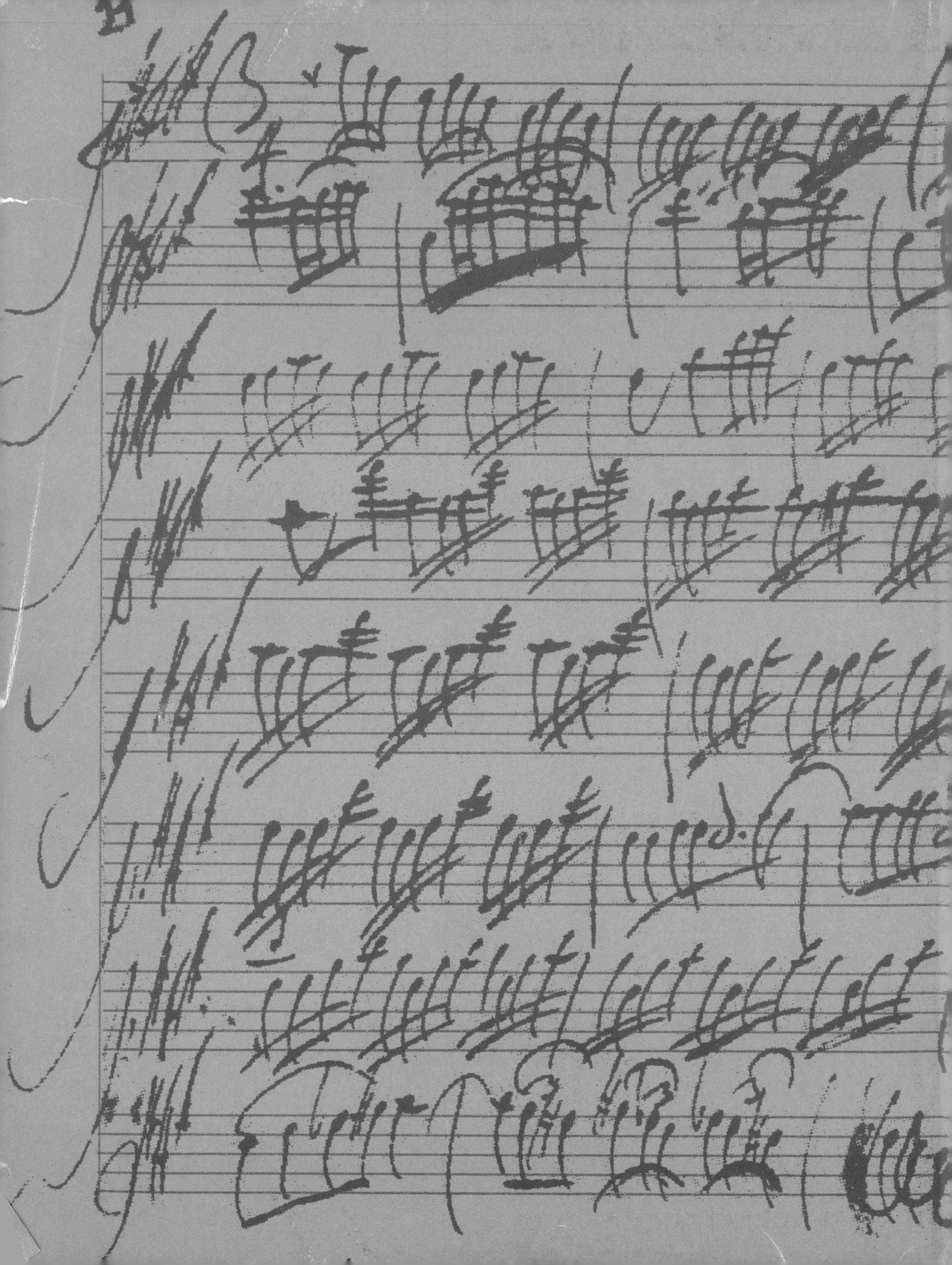